Annie and the Tiger

Scholastic Children's Books,
7-9 Pratt Street, London NW1 0AE, UK
A division of Scholastic Publications Ltd
London - New York - Toronto - Sydney - Auckland

First published by Scholastic Publications Ltd, 1992

This edition published by Scholastic Publications Ltd, 1995

Copyright © Kathy Henderson, 1992

ISBN 0 590 55322 4

Annie and the Tiger

Kathy Henderson

Annie was prowling
through the grass
in the park
when she met . . .

A tiger!

'I'm not scared of tigers,'
said Annie.
The tiger said, 'Miaow,'
and rubbed up against her.

Annie stroked the tiger
from the back of its head
all down its stripy back
and up its furry feather
of a tail.
The tiger purred.

But when Annie
tried to pick it up
the tiger ran away.

Annie ran after
the tiger.
Through the bushes,

under
the bench,

up a tree

and onto the wall.

Then the tiger
flicked its tail
and disappeared.

Annie
stomped home.
She was wet.
She was muddy.

She had a hole
in her trousers
and water
in her boots
and she didn't
have the tiger.

When she got in
she took off her boots,
she took off her trousers,
she took off her
squidgy soggy socks.

And when she looked round . . .

There was the tiger again
waving his tail
from the windowsill.

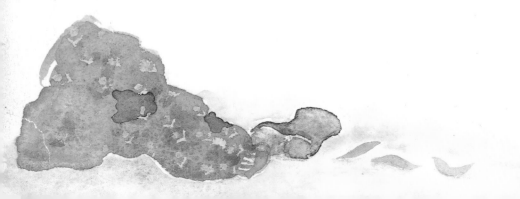